Holding onto Sunday

Also by Kathryn O. Galbraith

Katie Did!
illustrated by Ted Ramsey

Something Suspicious

Waiting for Jennifer
illustrated by Irene Trivas

Roommates
illustrated by Mark Graham

Roommates and Rachel
illustrated by Mark Graham

Look! Snow!
illustrated by Nina Montezinos

Roommates Again
illustrated by Mark Graham

(Margaret K. McElderry Books)

Hays ©95

Holding onto Sunday

Kathryn O. Galbraith
illustrated by Michael Hays

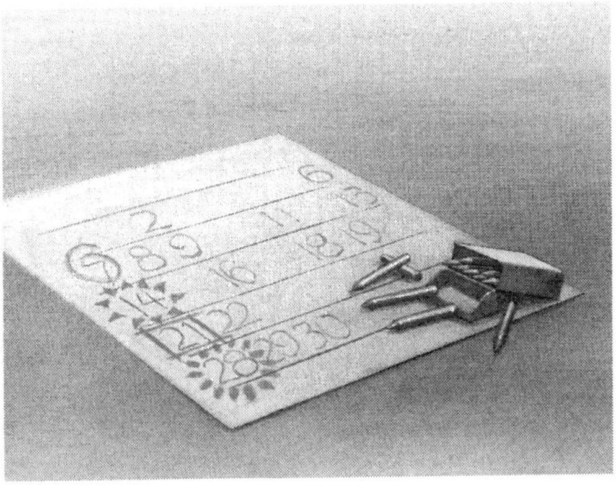

MARGARET K. MCELDERRY BOOKS

Margaret K. McElderry Books
An imprint of Simon & Schuster Children's Publishing Division
1230 Avenue of the Americas
New York, NY 10020

Designed by Nancy Williams
The text of this book is set in Aldine 721 BT.
The illustrations were done in pencil.
Printed in the United States of America
FIRST EDITION
10 9 8 7 6 5 4 3 2 1

Library of Congress Cataloging-in-Publication Data
Galbraith, Kathryn Osebold.
Holding onto Sunday / Kathryn O. Galbraith ; illustrated by Michael Hays.
p. cm.
Summary: Jemma's father always reserves Sunday as a special day to spend with his daughter.
ISBN 0-689-50623-6
[1. Fathers and daughters—Fiction. 2. Sunday—Fiction. 3. Dinosaurs—Fiction. 4. Museums—Fiction.] I. Hays, Michael, 1956– ill. II. Title.
PZ7.G1303Ho 1995
[Fic]—dc20 94-12796

In memory of my father
And once again to Steve

—K. O. G.

Chapter 1

On Sunday Jemma woke up early.

"Who's that?" Grandma called. "My little too-early bird?"

Jemma ran into the kitchen. She gave Grandma a good-morning hug.

"Is it time yet?" she asked.

"No, not yet," Grandma said.

Jemma sighed. On all the other days—Monday, Tuesday, Wednesday, Thursday, Friday, and sometimes even on Saturday—

Daddy had to go to work. He left early in the morning. He came home late at night.

But Sunday . . . Sunday was a special day. The best day. Jemma's favorite day of the whole week.

"Do you want some breakfast?" Grandma asked.

Jemma shook her head. She was hungry, but she didn't want breakfast. Not yet.

Jemma circled the table. She was too restless to sit. She nibbled on Grandma's cinnamon toast. She took a sip of Grandma's tea.

"Augh!" It was so bitter, it made her shiver.

"Oh, Jemma." Grandma smiled. "You know you never like it."

"I know," Jemma said. But every Sunday she had to try it again just to see.

Jemma leaned against Grandma's chair.

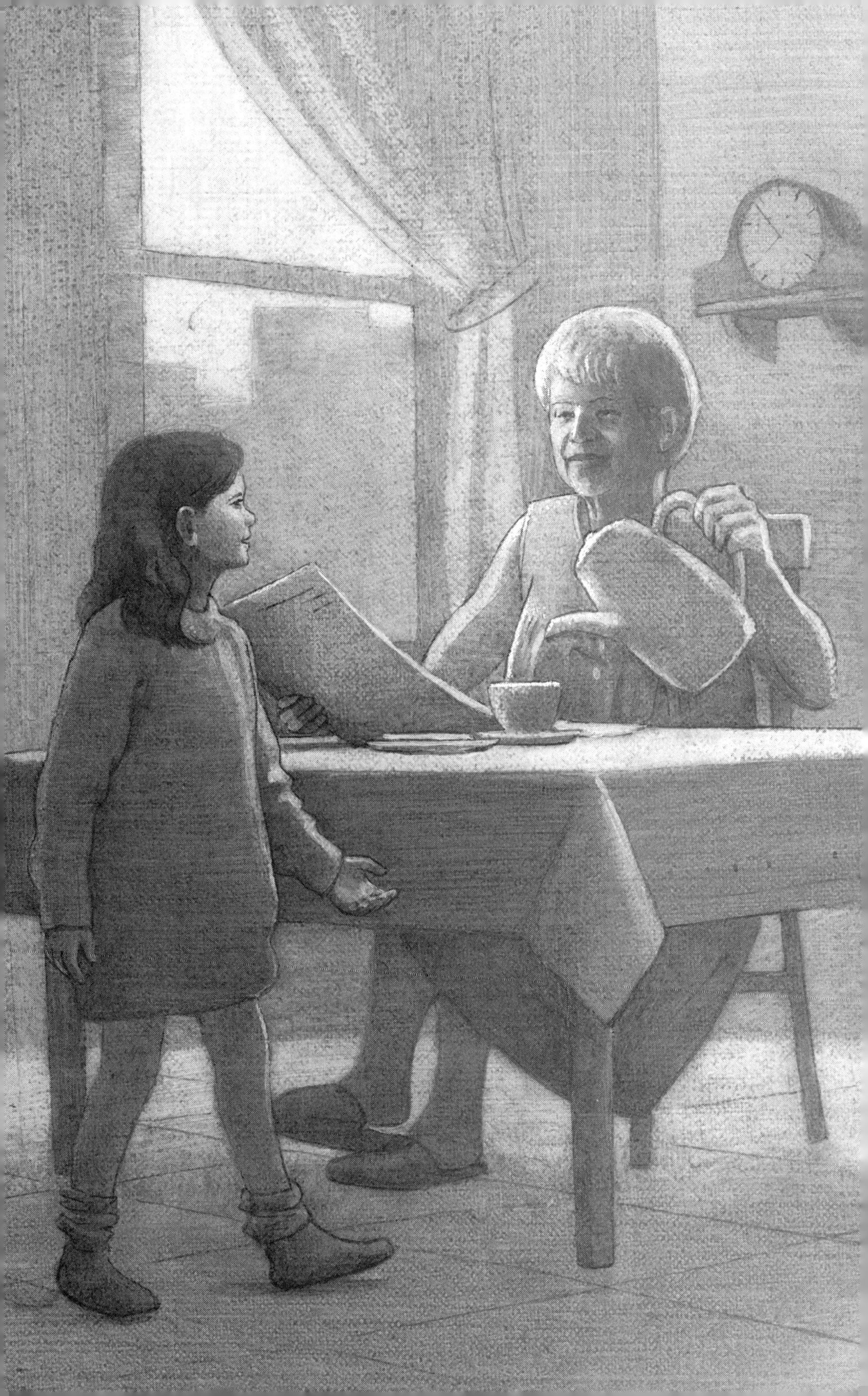

She played with the sugar bowl until Grandma rustled the newspaper at her.

"Is it time yet?" Jemma asked.

"Almost," Grandma said. "But first, go get dressed. And put some shoes on those feet."

On Sundays Jemma always wore her favorite everything.

Her favorite jeans. Rainbow sweater. Purple socks. And her favorite old shoes with their new purple laces.

Jemma wiggled her feet. Her new laces bounced. They bounced and danced all the way into the kitchen.

Tick, tick, tick went the old kitchen clock.

"Okay, now?" she asked.

Grandma looked up from the newspaper. Then she smiled. "Okay," she said. "Now."

Before Grandma even finished, Jemma was running down the hall.

Chapter 2

Jemma pushed open Daddy's bedroom door.

"Daddy," she called. "It's Sunday! It's time to get up."

Daddy didn't move, so Jemma stepped a little closer. "Hey! Daddy!"

Suddenly Daddy ROARED like a lion and reached out to grab her.

Jemma shrieked and jumped back. Then she laughed. Daddy had never caught her yet.

"What are we going to do today?" she called.

"Today we're going to tickle Jemma."

"Nooooo," Jemma shouted.

"All right," Daddy said. "Then we'll think of something else."

But what was that something going to be?

Before she could ask, Daddy threw back the covers.

"First things first," he said. "How about a little breakfast?"

Daddy always whistled when he cooked. Sometimes on Sunday he made pancakes or fried egg sandwiches. Sometimes he made hobo hash.

"Well, ladies," he asked, "what's it going to be today?"

"Pancakes!" Jemma said. "With lots and lots of syrup." She looked at Grandma.

"Oh, nothing for me," Grandma said. "I've already had my breakfast."

Jemma and Daddy smiled. That's what Grandma always said.

Then just like she always did, Grandma laughed. "But I guess I'll have another bite with you."

Right after breakfast, Daddy took a shower. Then he shaved. Jemma came in and watched while he made faces in the mirror.

Pat, pat, pat. Daddy patted aftershave all over his face.

"Now, where's Jemma?"

But Jemma was too quick for him.

She scooted out the door before he could pat, pat, pat it all over her.

"Grab your coat and grab your hat," Daddy sang after her. "We're going to paint the town—"

"Purple," Jemma yelled.

But wait! Was that rain on the window?

Jemma ran to look. Big, fat drops fell against the glass. "Oh, no!" Rain on Sunday! Her favorite day of the whole week. Now what were they going to do?

Chapter 3

Daddy came and stood at the window with Jemma. His coat sleeve brushed her cheek. He looked out at the rain and shook his head. "It's too wet for the park," he said. "Or even the zoo, but . . ."

He reached for her hand. Then he reached for his umbrella. "I guess we won't melt if we get a little wet."

"No, you're not that sweet," Grandma teased. "But don't forget your raincoat, Jemma."

Out in the hallway, Jemma ran ahead. She pushed the button for the elevator. When the elevator came, Daddy winked at her. "Lobby, please," he said.

Jemma giggled and pushed the L button. She never got tired of playing elevator.

Outside, Daddy and Jemma walked under Daddy's big umbrella. The rain pattered down. Jemma reached out her hand. She let the cool drops patter on her.

"Which way shall we go?" Daddy asked.

“Hmmm.” Jemma thought hard. “This way,” she said. “We can play Pick-a-Present.”

Jemma and Daddy walked slowly past the big store windows. They looked in every one.

“I pick . . . ”

Jemma picked a red bow tie and a wiggly, brown puppy for Daddy.

Then it was Daddy's turn.

"I pick . . ."

Daddy picked out a fancy dollhouse and a hat with feathers for Jemma.

"Oh, look," Jemma said. She pointed to a pair of black tap-dance shoes. "Let's pick those for Grandma!"

At the corner Jemma and Daddy stopped for the light. It was raining harder now. Jemma held her breath. Which way would they go? Right or left? Uptown or home?

Jemma didn't want to go home. Not yet. Not on Sunday.

"Let's go this way," she said. She pointed uptown.

Daddy thought for a minute. Then he smiled. "Okay. I know what we can do. We can look for dinosaurs."

"Really?" Jemma asked.

"Really," Daddy said.

As the wind tugged at their umbrella, Jemma and Daddy sailed uptown on a dinosaur hunt.

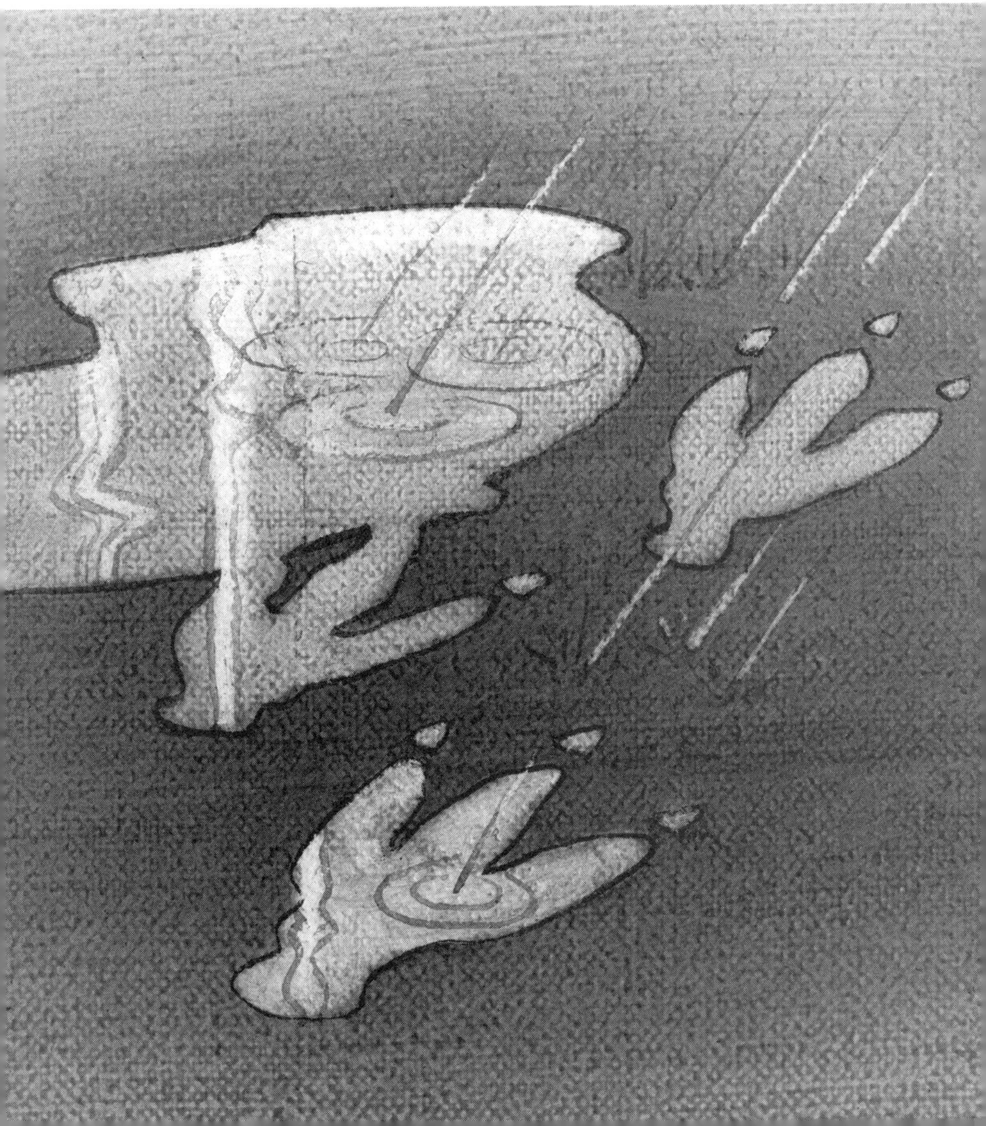

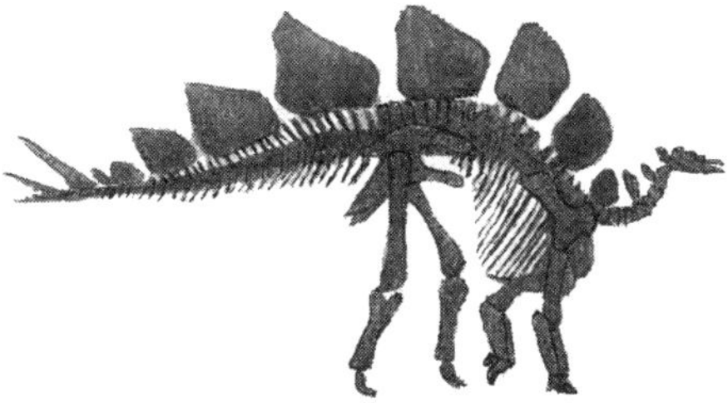

Chapter 4

"I didn't know there were dinosaurs *here,*" Jemma said. She looked up, up at the building in front of her. The Natural History Museum was as big as a castle.

"Well," Daddy said, "if there are any dinosaurs around, I bet this is where we'll find them."

Jemma and Daddy climbed the steep steps of the museum. Jemma counted out loud. "Thirteen, fourteen, fifteen, whew!"

In the lobby were two big bronze elephants. Jemma gave her favorite one a pat.

Then Daddy squeezed her hand. "Look over there." He pointed to a sign:

NEW EXHIBIT—DINOSAURS THIS WAY

Jemma and Daddy followed the sign. They walked slowly past stuffed alligators and crocodiles.

"And snakes!" Jemma said. "I remember that big one."

Daddy and Jemma walked and walked until they turned a corner and—

"Ohhhh!" Jemma tipped her head back and stared.

A *Tyrannosaurus rex* stared back. It was huge. Huger than huge. It looked down at Jemma with empty eyes. It grinned at her with fierce, sharp teeth.

Jemma shivered with delight. "What would happen if it reached out and grabbed me?" she whispered.

"I'd reach out and grab you back," Daddy said. *"Like this!"*

And he caught her up into a big, warm hug.

Jemma and Daddy looked at all the

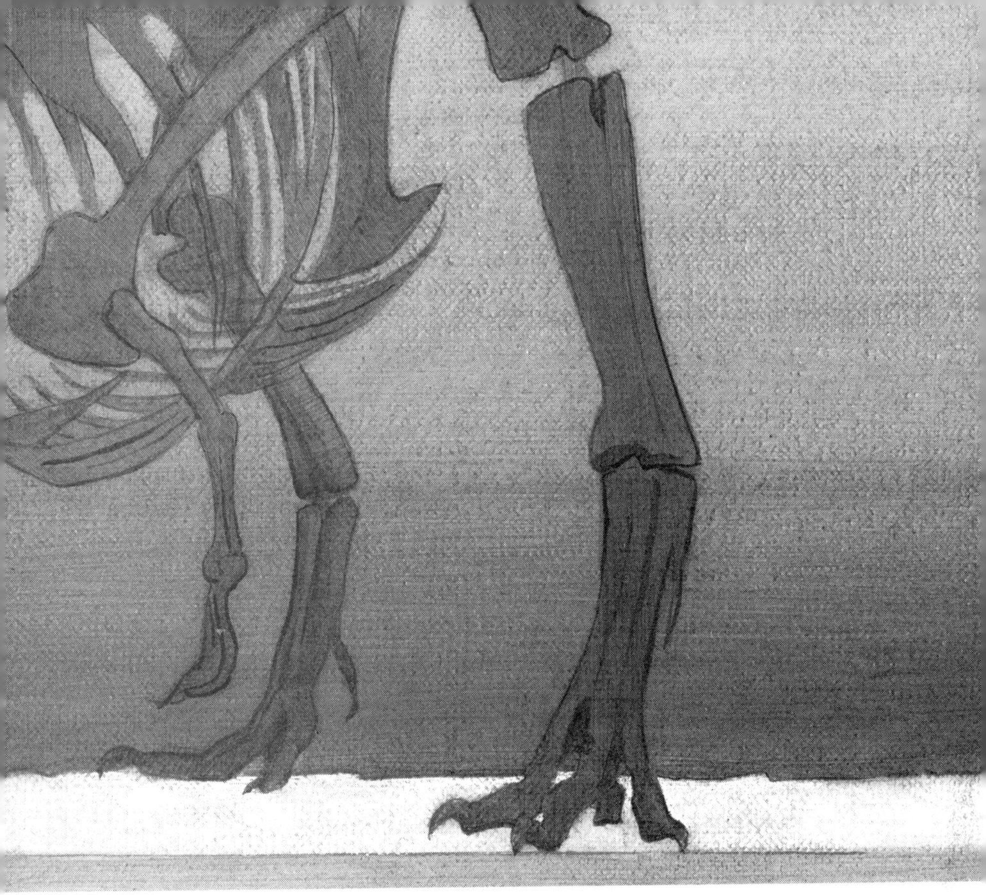

dinosaur bones. They looked at dinosaur footprints. They looked at dinosaur eggs.

After they had looked at everything twice, Daddy said, "You know what? Dinosaurs make me hungry."

Jemma didn't want to leave, but dinosaurs made her hungry, too.

Slowly Jemma and Daddy walked back to the lobby. Jemma patted her favorite elephant good-bye.

"I bet we see him again soon," Daddy said.

Outside, the rain had turned to mist. Together Jemma and Daddy climbed down the steep steps.

Jemma counted out loud. "Thirteen, fourteen, fifteen, whew!"

"Aha!" Daddy said. He pointed to the hot dog man and his cart. "I see food."

Jemma and Daddy shared a hot dog, half with mustard, half without.

On the way home, they talked about dinosaurs. They talked about puddles and rainbows, too.

Suddenly Jemma remembered something else. Something special to tell Daddy. But she wouldn't tell him now, she decided. Not yet. She gave a little hop. Then a spin. No, she'd wait and tell him right after dinner.

Chapter 5

Daddy unlocked the apartment door. "Mmmm." He sniffed the air. "I smell chicken. Roast chicken."

Jemma sniffed the air, too. "I smell potatoes," she said.

"I smell lettuce," Daddy said.

Jemma giggled. "I smell—"

"Raindrops," Grandma said. She gave them both a kiss.

Jemma helped Grandma set the table.

Jemma put out the white china plates. Grandma put out the tall water glasses.

Daddy mashed the potatoes until they were smooth. “Smooth as silk,” Daddy said.

During dinner Jemma told Grandma all about the dinosaurs. But Jemma didn’t tell Daddy her special news. Not yet.

After Sunday dinner Daddy always did the dishes.

"Can I help?" Jemma asked.

As Daddy washed the dishes, Jemma dried them.

"Guess what?" she said. She couldn't wait any longer. "I'm going to be a butterfly in

Miss Jackie's recital. And I get to wear wings," she added. "Blue wings. Grandma's going to make them.

"And watch," she said. "This is the butterfly waltz."

Jemma danced across the floor. She remembered almost every hop and spin.

"Bravo!" Daddy clapped and clapped.

Jemma felt her face grow warm. "And you know what else?" she said. "Miss Jackie said everyone can come and watch. Grandma's going to be there." She looked up at him. "Can you come, too?"

"Absolutely, positively," Daddy said.

Jemma let out her breath and smiled. When Daddy said, "Absolutely, positively," it meant yes. Yes for sure.

When the last dish had been put away, Grandma said, "Bath time, Jemma."

Jemma sighed. Sunday was almost over.

After Jemma's bath, Daddy asked, "What story do you want to hear tonight?"

Jemma looked through all her books. She chose the biggest, fattest one. "I want to hear this one," she said.

Sitting in the nest of Daddy's arm, Jemma listened as the words rumbled against her ear.

When Daddy turned the last page, they both sighed. Sunday was over.

Daddy tucked Jemma into bed. He gave her a kiss and turned off the light. "Good night, Butterfly," he called softly.

In the quiet darkness, Jemma counted on her fingers. Monday, Tuesday, Wednesday, Thursday, Friday, Saturday . . . Sunday.

Holding onto Sunday, she drifted off to sleep.